Phantom Feast

Jacques Duquennoy

ORCHARD BOOKS

Freddy has invited
all his phantom friends
to a special feast.

Here they all are in the huge dining-room of his castle.

But where's Freddy ?

He's busy in the kitchen.

Here he comes, at last.

Would anyone like a drink?

Yes, please!

Oh dear! The tray seems to be stuck.

Ah. That's better.

Try one of my special concoctions. It's a secret recipe.

Mmm...I think I'll try this one.

Whooa! Steady!

Mmm, it's not bad.　　　In fact, it's delicious!

Freddy, these drinks are amazing!

Just wait till you've tried my pumpkin soup.
Careful, it's hot!

Mmm...it's wonderful!

And now for the salmon. Lovely pink salmon!

Then salad...

And cheese.

Freddy, what a wonderful feast!

There's still pudding to come.

And here it is...Freddy the Chef's Special Surprise!

Mmm...it looks delicious.

Wow, it *is* delicious.

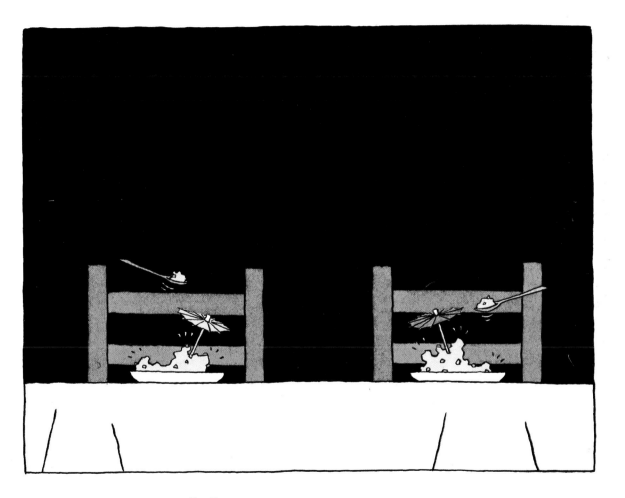

My favourite ice-cream.

Oh look!

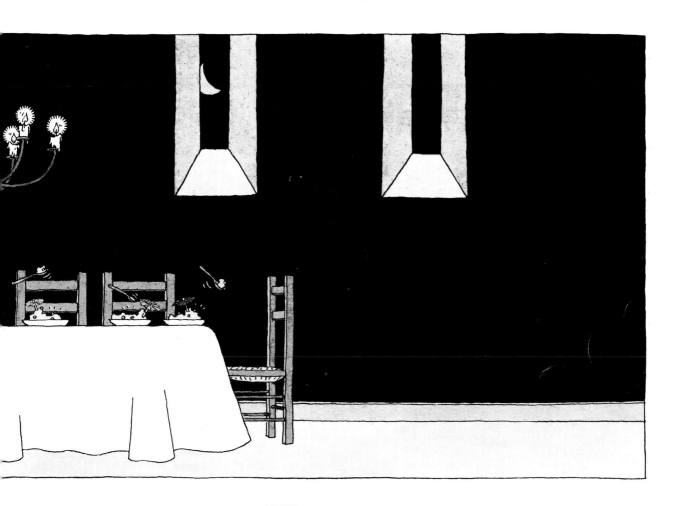

We're invisible!

This is great!
Let's clear the table...

Whoops! Mind the step!

We'll give you a hand
with the washing-up.

And the drying-up.

Anyone for coffee?

Mmm...

What good coffee.

And to finish off, a nice bowl of warm milk.

Freddy, that was a fabulous feast.

But where *is* Freddy?

He can't still be in the kitchen?

Freddy! Where are you?

BOO!

Phantom fright!
Hee, hee!